Elisabeth Felten

KIDNAPPED

Elisabeth Felten is an associate professor of business at DeSales University. She is the founder of a post-secondary academic program for adults with intellectual disabilities and autism. Her interest in writing books for adults with low literacy started when she couldn't find appropriate books for her students and summer book club. Elisabeth is currently pursuing an MFA in creative writing.

First published by Gemma in 2025.

www.gemmamedia.org

Printed in the United States of America

978-1-956476-48-4

Library of Congress Cataloging-in Publication Data available.

Cover by Laura Shaw Design

Named after the brightest star in the North-
ern Crown, Gemma is a nonprofit organiza-
tion that helps new readers acquire English
language literacy skills with relevant, engaging
books, eBooks, and audiobooks. Always orig-
inal, never adapted, these stories introduce
adults and young adults to the life-changing
power of reading.

Open Door

For Isabella

I was kidnapped. Legally.

I was in my room listening to a book on my iPad. My aide gave me a shower and fed me breakfast. I have help doing these things because I have cerebral palsy. That means my body doesn't move the way I want. But other than that, I'm just like other people. I read books and play video games. My favorite band is the Rolling Stones. They're old, I know. Their music makes me think of my parents. They played them a lot when I was a kid.

I live in a group home with men like me. We were going to a baseball game in the afternoon. I was wearing my favorite baseball shirt. Our team,

The Great Lake Loons, were playing the Dayton Dragons. Game day is the best. I love eating hot dogs and drinking Coke on a hot summer day. Games are more fun when you are with friends.

I was in my room waiting until it was time to leave. Loud noises came from the hall. My aide yelled, "Sir, please wait."

The door to my room opened fast. It hit the wall with a loud bang. Nick, my older brother, walked in. I jumped. It took me a minute to see it was him. It has been ten years since I saw him.

"Hi, Sam. You are coming to live with me in Minnesota." He grabbed my wheelchair and turned me quickly. My iPad smashed to the ground. The sound made him stop and look around.

He grabbed my trash can and emptied the bag on the floor. He put some of my clothes into the empty bag. Then he rolled me out the door. It happened so fast. My aides just stood there. They didn't know what to do.

Nick is my legal guardian. He makes the rules even if I don't like it. Because of cerebral palsy, I can't speak. But I have a lot to say. As Nick rolled me out of my house, I hit the "NO" sticker on my wheelchair tray.

No! No! No!

But Nick is my guardian. I can't stop him.

Chapter 2

We've been driving for hours. Minnesota is seven hundred miles away from Saginaw. Nick hasn't said a word. I don't know why he's moving me. I love my home. Michigan is where we grew up. There's nothing for me in Minnesota.

We stop for gas and Nick leaves me in the car. The summer sun bakes me like a bug in a jar. I yell but no one hears me...or they don't care. By the time Nick comes back, my head and throat hurt from yelling. He puts a bottle of water in the cup holder. Cold water drips slowly down the side. There it sits, teasing me.

Nick speeds onto the highway. I try to calm myself. I listen to the hum of the road. But when we change lanes, I fall over. I'm now stuck with my head against the window. It smacks the glass with every bump we hit. Hot, thick air from the one open window burns my face. My ears buzz. My head feels dizzy.

Help me. Please. Someone, help me.

Nick drives a small old Honda Civic hatchback. I'm six feet, four inches and too tall to be sitting in the back seat. Why am I even in the back seat? I'm twenty-three, not a little kid. My legs hurt. The door handle cuts into my knee. I try to move my knee to open the door. I wish I could roll myself out.

From a plastic bag, Nick pulls out snacks. He eats the chips right in front of me. He hasn't changed. All he eats is junk food and he never shares. I hope he chokes.

Next, Nick takes a hot dog from the bag. *Pop* goes the can. I should be at the baseball game right now. That hot dog and Coke should be mine. My mouth is dry as dust. That cold pop sure would taste good. The smell of that hot dog makes my stomach rumble. Nick licks ketchup off his greedy fingers. I want to throw up.

I try to think of something else. From here, I can see a bald spot on the back of Nick's head. He didn't have that when I saw him ten years ago. Nick is in his early thirties. He is too young to be losing his hair. I laugh. Nick turns and gives me an ugly look.

I laugh louder.

Chapter 3

Nick's little house is as ugly as the broken fence in the yard. The bushes are brown. The door is brown. The stairs would be brown, but the paint has come off. The porch hangs crooked. There's no ramp for my wheelchair.

Nick opens the car door, and I almost fall out. As he pushes me up, he pinches my arm. He gives me a fake smile like when we were kids. Then, without telling me, he pulls me up over his shoulder like a child.

I'm so skinny you can see my bones, but Nick is weak. He grunts under my weight. He is much shorter than me, but puffy and round. With each step, my feet kick him in the knees. That makes me smile. I open my mouth wide. Spit runs onto the old t-shirt he's had since high school.

I won't make this easy for you, brother.

I see an older lady in a housecoat coming toward us.

"Nick! Hello!"

Nick turns fast. I can't see the lady anymore. "Hi, Lanie. I'd love to talk, but my hands are full."

"Here, let me help you." She rushes to the door and opens it. The door is not locked. Of course, why lock an ugly house like this?

"Nick, is this your brother?"

"Yes. This is Sam," he grunts as he takes me into the house.

"Hello, Sam! It's nice to meet you."

I'm embarrassed that this woman is talking to my butt. I look like a child over his shoulder. Why didn't Nick put me in my wheelchair?

Inside, he drops me onto the sofa. It makes me pee. There is a large wet spot on the front of my pants. Lanie walks in and sees it. Her eyes grow wide. My face fills with heat. Lanie grabs a towel from the kitchen.

"Sam, you live in Michigan, right?" She looks at Nick who is just standing there. "What a long drive you had. You must be tired." She moves toward me like...

No! Is this stranger going to clean me up? Are you kidding me?

"I got it, Lanie." Nick steps between us and takes the towel. "Thanks for your help. We're fine here." Nick takes her to the door.

No, wait! I don't want Lanie to clean me up, but I do want her to stay. I yell *"stop,"* but with my cerebral palsy, it's just a sound.

"Thanks for coming Lanie."

"I can—" Nick shuts the door on her and locks it.

"Crazy cat lady." Nick drops the towel next to me.

"Home sweet home, Sam. Goodnight."

And with that, he walks down the hall. I hear the TV turn on. He's watching a baseball game.

Angry tears run down my face. I guess I'm sleeping in wet pants tonight. I would yell, but that would make Nick happy. He likes that I'm out here help-less. I'm not going to give him what he wants.

I look over at the kitchen. Fast food wrappers cover the counter. My stomach rumbles.

Just then I hear a noise. Lanie is tapping gently on the porch window. I look her in the eye. She points to herself, then the house next door. She says something I can't hear. She points at me and then back at her. She smiles, waves, and walks away.

I need to find a way to talk to Lanie.

Chapter 4

Tap, tap, tap.

The sun is shining through the porch window. I'm still in the same place Nick dropped me last night. I'm trapped in this ugly little house.

"Hello? Nick? Sam? I brought you some banana bread for breakfast. Fresh from the oven!" Lanie sings from the porch. Her voice is so bright and happy. She looks in the window and sees me. Her mouth falls open.

Yes, Lanie. I've been on this couch all night. In wet pants.

She knocks harder, faster.

Nick's slow footsteps come down the hall. He walks into the living room and rubs his eyes. He looks surprised.

Did you forget I was here, brother?

He sniffs and makes a face. The room smells like pee.

Nick opens the door, just a little. Lanie tries to come in, but Nick stops her. She tries to look past him, trying to see me.

"Good morning, Nick. I brought you and Sam some fresh baked banana bread. Can I come in?" Her voice is different now. It sounds shaky.

"Thanks, Lanie. That's nice of you, but it's not a good time."

It has been a day since I've eaten. Warm banana bread sounds so good.

"Yes, please!" I yell, but to them, it's just sounds.

My brother's cell phone rings.

"I need to take a call, Lanie. Can you come back later? Thank you." He pushes her out with the door as he closes it. Lanie looks at me through the window again. Her face shows worry. She points to herself, then the bread, then to me. She nods "yes" and gives a thumbs up. She waves and walks away.

"Hello. Nita Rhodes? Who are you?" Nick hits the speaker button. He walks into the kitchen. As he talks, he takes something out of the refrigerator.

I know that voice coming through the phone. Nita, my favorite aide! It's Monday. She must have just started work for the day.

"I was surprised that Sam was moved. Did anyone go over his care plan with you?" I laugh. Nita is using her work voice, not her fun voice.

"I don't need a care plan to take care of my brother, Ms. Rhodes."

"I know Mr. Jackson, but there are ways we feed Sam so he doesn't choke." I can tell she is mad.

"I know my own brother, Ms. Rhodes."

No, you don't. He never calls or visits me. He doesn't send me a birthday present. Not even a Christmas card.

"I went through the list of Sam's things. Most of them are still here. Like his iPad. Sam uses it to talk." Nita's voice is getting louder.

"We will get along just fine, Ms. Rhodes."

I start yelling so Nita can hear me. She will know something is wrong. She will fix this and bring me home.

"See, Ms. Rhodes? You can hear how happy Sam is to be here."

Liar.

"Can I talk to him? I took care of him for so many years. We laughed a lot. Your brother is a funny guy, Mr. Jackson. I would like to say goodbye." Nita is using her "I can play this game, too" voice.

"I will tell him you called, Ms. Rhodes." And with that, he ends the call.

I know Nita. She is smart. She won't let him do this to me.

Nick has a spoon and a bowl of something green. He puts it in my mouth. It's lime Jello. I'm going to throw up. I hate Jello. I spit it into his face.

I won't make this easy, brother.

Chapter 5

Nick puts the rest of the Jello in the sink.

"It's time to get ready, Sam. We are going to the Social Security office."

What are you up to, brother?

He puts me over his shoulder like a baby again. In the bathroom, Nick runs water for a bath. At my home in Michigan, I take showers. My aides run the hot water first to warm up the room. They put on some Rolling Stones music. We laugh and say it's my "spa time." It feels so good when they rub my head as they wash my hair.

Nick puts me into a tub that's not warm enough. He scrubs harder than he should. He doesn't cover my face as he washes my hair. Shampoo burns my eyes. Soap runs into my mouth, and I cough.

Nick lets the water out from the tub and leaves the room. I shake from the cold. The front door opens.

No, no, no. Is he going to leave me in here? I close my eyes and think what to do.

Thud!

I jump. Nick drops the trash bag of my clothes on the floor.

He pulls me out of the tub from under my arms. My knee hits the side. *Ouch.* I land on the floor with a thud. *Just like a trash bag.* I'm naked on the cold tile.

Nick is rolling me side to side as he dries me. It would be so much easier if

I was in a shower chair. He grunts as he lifts my hips to put on my pants.

"Come on, Sam. Help me here."

Help? Sure, I'll help! I wave my arms making it hard for him to put on my shirt. He says some bad words.

Nick starts shaving me. Right there on the floor. I try not to move. He uses short quick strokes that hurt my skin.

Is this how you shave yourself, brother? Why is it so hard to be nice to me? What did I ever do to you?

A sharp pain shoots across my cheek. Blood runs down my neck. He sticks bits of toilet paper on the cut. It stings.

Finally, he's done. I hurt, but it feels good to be clean. The smell of sweat and pee are gone. My clothes smell like home.

I feel human again.

Chapter 6

A few hours later, we park at the Social Security office. Nick gets my wheelchair out of the car. I'm happy that he is not going to carry me again. He rolls me up to the office door but can't get me in.

Hello, brother! See that blue button? The one with the wheelchair on it? It opens the door. For real! Try it!

A nice man comes over and opens the door. I want to say "thank you," but he won't understand my voice. Nick says nothing. It makes me mad. I don't want people to think I'm like him.

"Can I help you?" A security guard comes up to us. He looks me in the eye. I hit the YES sticker on my wheelchair tray. Nick sees it and steps in front of me.

"Good morning," Nick says in a fake work voice. "I have an appointment for my brother, Sam Jackson."

"You can check in over there." The security guard points to the wall.

Nick leaves me in the middle of the room. He taps the screen, takes a ticket and sits down. The security guard looks at Nick, then at me. He walks over to Nick.

"Sir. There are seats by the window. You and your brother can sit together."

Nick's face turns red. He pushes me over to the window and sits down. He peels the YES sticker off my tray. He starts on the NO, but a loud voice comes through the room.

"Ticket A15 to window six. Ticket A15 to window six."

Nick jumps up and pushes me down the hallway. He carefully pulls my wheelchair up to the desk at window six. He sits next to me and puts his hand on my shoulder. Nick smiles at the agent.

Chapter 7

"How can I help you today?" asks the agent.

"Hello, I am Nick Jackson. This is my brother, Sam. He gets money from Social Security. He just moved to Minnesota. How can we have his money sent to my house?"

Ah. Now I see why he moved me. This is about money. I should have known.

The agent looks me in the eye.

"Good morning, Mr. Jackson," the agent says to me. "How are you today?"

"Fine, thank you," Nick answers.

"I'm glad, but I was talking to your brother, sir."

Ha! Take that, brother!

"Sam doesn't talk." I don't like the sound of Nick's voice. He's mad.

The agent looks at me again. "How are you today, Mr. Jackson?"

I yell and hit the NO sticker on my wheelchair tray. I don't think the agent can see it.

"Are you Sam's Representative Payee?" the agent asks Nick.

"I don't know what that means. I'm his legal guardian. Is that the same thing?" Nicks smiles again.

"No," the agent says gently. "The Social Security office chooses a Representative Payee. It is a person who takes care of Sam's money."

"How can I be that person?"

I yell and hit the NO sticker on my wheelchair tray again. Nick smiles and puts his hand on mine.

"Do you have papers for both of you?"

"Yes, sir." Nick gives the papers to the agent. "This shows I am Sam's legal guardian."

The agent asks Nick many questions. Did he ever break the law? Did he spend time in jail? Has he taken anyone's Social Security money before? Nick looks sick. He moves in his chair.

"No, sir. I haven't," Nick looks down as he talks. He taps his foot.

"Everything looks good here." The agent turns to Nick. "The money will come in about six weeks."

I yell as loud as I can. I hit the NO over and over again. Nick puts his arm around me like a hug so I can't move. His eyes are wide.

"Six weeks?"

"Yes, that's how long it takes. I have Sam's new address. Next, you must open a bank account in Sam's name. Once a year, you will have to show how his money was spent."

Nick moves in his chair again.

"I didn't know it took so long." Nick's foot is tapping faster.

"Yes. We must protect the people getting Social Security money. Is there anything else I can help you with today?"

I yell again. Nick pats my arm and smiles.

"No, thank you. We have everything we need." Nick stands up and turns my wheelchair.

I hit the NO again and again as he rolls me out. When we get to the car, he rips off the NO and throws it on the ground. Nick makes a phone call.

"Hey man, it's going to be a few more weeks until I can get you your money."

I see what you are doing, brother. It's not going to work. Someone will stop you.

When we get back to Nick's house, there's a basket of banana bread waiting at the front door.

Chapter 8

Nick is making quesadillas for lunch. The sweet smell of the corn makes my stomach rumble. The oil pops as he flips the tortilla. Yum! All that warm cheese makes my mouth water.

On the table is a picture of Nick and his girlfriend. She looks pretty and too good for someone like Nick. I wonder where she is. Nick looks happy in the picture. The move to Minnesota was good for him.

He couldn't wait to leave Michigan. Nick's best friend moved to Minnesota in high school. When Nick turned eighteen, he followed the friend there. I didn't care if he left. Nick and I were never close. He's been gone fifteen years now.

My parents adopted me when Nick was ten. I don't think Nick wanted a brother. He liked being an only child. It's not easy having a brother with special needs. My parents spent most of their time taking care of me. I went to the doctor a lot. Nick was left out. I don't blame him for leaving.

I look at Nick and see his bald spot again. The rest of his dark oily hair is getting thin. He is wearing old gray sweatpants. One dirty slipper has a hole in the toe. He looks different from this morning. At the Social Security office, he wore nice pants and a clean shirt. But nice clothes can't hide how ugly he is inside.

Nick puts the quesadillas onto plates. He pours some salsa on the side. Oh, these are going to be good! He takes two cans of beer out of the refrigerator. He puts the food and drinks on the table in front of me. The Minnesota Twins baseball game is on TV. Just two brothers watching a game together and drinking beer. This is nice. Maybe Nick *does* want to live with me.

Then, Nick pops open a beer and starts eating.

Hello? Over here, brother. It's me, Sam. The one sitting right next to you. How about some food for me?

Does he forget that I need help to eat? I call out to him, but he's too busy watching TV. Salsa drips down his shirt. Looking at him makes me sick.

When Nick is done eating, he looks over at me, then at the plate of food. The quesadilla is cold. He puts some in my mouth. The cheese is hard and the tortilla dry. Aides mix my food with water so I don't choke. I cough and food sprays onto Nick's face. He jumps back and yells. It was an accident but I'm glad it happened. He gets a glass of water and starts to pour it in my mouth.

No, no. I use a water bottle.

Aides squeeze drinks into my mouth. My mouth opens and closes on its own. I can't stop it. They wait until my mouth opens to spray the drink. I don't choke that way.

Nick keeps trying to feed me. It's a mess. Food falls in my lap. Water runs down my chin. My shirt is wet. I can't help but cry.

Nick's head drops into his hands. When he gets up, he has tears in his eyes, too. He walks away, and I hear his door slam. The TV in his bedroom turns on. The sound gets louder. I call to him. He didn't feed me as a kid. It's not so easy. I wish he talked with my aides before taking me here.

An hour later, he comes out wearing a baseball shirt. He walks out the front door, starts his car, and drives away.

Chapter 9

It's dark when Nick returns. He smells like beer and smoke. I don't know how long I've been on the couch. At some time, I fell over. My face is in the pillow. My back hurts. I've also wet myself again. I am so sick of sitting in pee.

Nick's lip curls when he smells the room.

"I bought you diapers." He throws the pack onto the couch.

Diapers? I don't need diapers. I need aides. I need my iPad so I can say when I need help. I need my bathroom wheelchair. It has a hole in the seat so I can go to the bathroom. I need to be treated like an adult.

Nick puts his keys down and gets a drink of water. He walks down the hall. The water turns on in the bathroom. Great. I won't see him for the rest of the night.

But then he comes back. He's wearing those ugly gray sweatpants again. He pulls me over his shoulder. I poop. I can't help it. It's been two days since I was on a toilet. Nick curses.

Do you think I like this, brother?

Nick lays me on the bathroom floor and takes off my clothes. He tries to wipe me with toilet paper. It doesn't work. He puts me in the tub. Here we go again.

At least the water is warmer. It turns brown as Nick washes my body. Nick lets the water out of the tub. I don't feel clean. He fills the tub and washes me again. I wish he knew that showers are easier.

Nick puts me in a diaper. I don't like it. I'm not a baby. But I am clean and dry. He carries me to a bedroom down the hall and puts me in bed. He puts a pillow under my head. It looks like he's been crying.

I wonder what has changed.

Chapter 10

The small shadow on the wall says it's lunch time. I've been lying in this bed all day. There is a glass of water and some banana bread next to me. But I can't reach it. Or feed myself.

I've called out to Nick many times. The house is quiet. I can see Lanie's house. She is standing at her window. I wave my arms as fast as I can.

Please see me, Lanie. Please come over.

She moves away from the window. I hope that means she's coming. From the bed I can see the clouds. They remind me of walks with Nita, my favorite aide. We used to go to Hoyt Park, the Saginaw Riverwalk, and the Saginaw River lighthouse. She would sing the Rolling Stones with me as we walked.

"Hey, you! Get off of my cloud."

We would point at each other and laugh. She also took me to see funny shows at the Temple Theater. It's a very fancy theater from the 1920s. The walls are painted gold. Fancy gold lights hang from the ceiling. After the show, we'd visit the museum. There are lots of old movie posters and other things in there.

My daydream is stopped by a knock at the door.

Lanie!

I yell and hope she hears me. The knock goes on for a few minutes and then...stops.

The sun moves over the house. The room is gray. As the hours go by, I get angry. Nita says being angry only hurts yourself. I try to be happy. But it's hard right now. I don't want to be here. I make up a new song.

"Hey, hey, Nick, Nick.
Get off of my cloud.
Don't hang around.
Because two's a crowd.
On my cloud."

My arms and head move as I sing. For a short time, it works. I'm happy.

I see Lanie at her window again. Can she see me? I call out and try to move closer to her. Back and forth I roll, waving my arms. It's working! I'm at the side of the bed.

Thud.

I hit the floor. This was not the plan. Now I'm stuck.

To pass the time, I count to a hundred. Then backward to one. I play baseball games in my head. I think of Nita. We had so much fun. I miss her.

It's late when Nick comes home. He smells like beer and smoke again. His face is cut up. His eyes are black and blue. His lip is puffy. What happened to him?

"Sorry, Sam. I didn't think I would be gone so long." His voice sounds sad.

Nick changes the diaper I'm wearing. He moves me to the couch. A bag of fast food is on the table. Gently, he puts small bites in my mouth.

Chapter 11

Someone is knocking on the door again. It's a loud, hard knock this time. Whoever it is wants us to know they are there. Nick moves slowly down the hallway. I hear the door open.

"Good morning. I'm here to see Sam Jackson."

"He's sleeping. Who are you?"

"I'm from Washington County Human Services. I would like to talk with Sam."

"Sam doesn't talk."

"I understand. But I still need to see him. I came yesterday. No one was home. Did you get the note I left in your door?"

"Oh, right. Yes, come in. I will get Sam."

I hear Nick coming down the hallway.

"Good morning, Sam. There's a woman here who wants to talk with you."

I think this is the most he's said to me since he took me from my home. He's carrying me now—the right way. I'm in his arms like a firefighter. We walk into the living room. He sits me on the couch.

"Good morning, Sam. My name is Tanya Woods. I'm a social worker with the County. Did you just move to Minnesota? How do you like it so far?"

Like it? No! I yell and move my body. I kick the coffee table.

Nick jumps up and quickly moves the table back into place.

"He didn't mean it. Sometimes his legs just move like that." Nick looks scared.

"I see your brother was carrying you, Sam. Do you have a wheelchair?"

I move my body side to side. I hit my hand on my leg. I hope she gets it. I need my iPad to talk.

"Yes," Nick says. "It's in the car."

"Sam may feel better in his chair." Tanya smiles at me.

I yell again, hitting my hand on my leg. Tanya looks me in the eye.

"Uh, yeah. I guess." Nick has his head down.

"Great. Let's get it now. I can help you get it from the car."

"I can get it myself." Nick leaves the house.

"Now that we're alone," Tanya says, "Nita Rhodes called us. She is worried about you. She said you left without your things. She says you need your iPad to talk." Tanya takes some paper from her bag. "I brought a YES and NO paper so we can talk."

She puts a paper with a large YES on my left leg and a NO on my right.

"Do you feel safe here, Sam?"

I move my right arm. *NO.*

Nick is on the porch. I hear the wheelchair bang up the steps.

"I'm going to help you, Sam," Tanya says, just as Nick opens the door.

"Great." Tanya stands up. "Let's get Sam into his chair."

Tanya and Nick put me into my wheelchair. It feels good to be sitting up. Tanya puts the tray on my lap. She puts the YES and NO signs on it. Nick's eyes open wide.

"Do you like your wheelchair, Sam?"

I smile. My left arm goes toward the YES. Tanya smiles. Nick runs his hand through his hair. Now that I can talk, he's in trouble.

Tanya puts her hand on my shoulder.

"I want Sam to get what he needs. I will make some calls. Please call the County about getting Sam money for food and bills. Here is the number."

Tanya writes something on a piece of paper. She gives it to Nick. His eyes light up. It's like he is holding gold. *Money*—just what Nick wants.

"Thank you, Ms. Woods. I will do that right away."

"Sam, it was nice to meet you. I will come back again soon."

Nita called her. It won't be long until I'm going home.

Nick slams the door. The look in his eyes scares me.

"It's always about you, Sammie boy." Nick spits as he talks. "You've only been here two days and people are coming to see you."

I've seen this look in Nick's eyes when we were kids. My parents would tell him to say goodbye or good night to me. He would smile, then pinch my back hard while he gave me a hug. I can still feel it all these years later.

"Everything is always about you, Sam. Your doctors. Trips to the hospital. Special schools. All the money went to you. I couldn't even get a video game console. Mom and Dad gave you a trust fund. But not me."

Ah. The trust fund. That's what this is about. First, he tried to get my Social Security money. Now he wants the money from my special needs trust.

Good luck, brother.

My parents left last year to work in a small church in Peru. They always wanted to do it. I wanted them to do it. I'm proud that I helped make their dreams come true.

When I was eighteen years old, I asked to live on my own. We found a great group home. There are people my age and great aides like Nita. My parents knew I was happy and doing well. They thought it might be time to do something for themselves. They sold their house and all their stuff. The money went into a special needs trust for me. Nick got some to buy this house. I was sad that my parents left but knew I would be OK. Well, until now.

My parents made Nick my legal guardian. They wanted me to be safe if something happened while they were gone. I didn't think much about it. My group home takes care of everything. Nick didn't need to do anything at all. Now, I wish my parents were here.

Nick was never good with money. As a kid, he spent money on all the shiny new things. He was also lazy. Other kids washed dishes in the Supper

Club or had jobs at a store. Nick just sat on the couch and watched TV. My parents didn't make him work. I think they felt bad. It's not always easy having a brother with cerebral palsy. They gave him money whenever he asked. If they ever said "no," he cried. If he said "It's not fair," my parents just gave him what he wanted. Except that video game console. It wasn't because of money. My parents didn't like video games. They thought those games made kids do bad things. It's the only thing they ever said "no" to for Nick. I don't know why he blames me for it.

My parents love Nick, but they are smart. They put an accountant in charge of the special needs trust. It's not easy to get money from it. Nick will never control my money.

Nick gives me a mean look again. He rips up the YES and NO papers from Tanya. Into the trash they go. Nick stomps off to his bedroom and turns on the TV.

Chapter 13

I'm so glad the social worker came yesterday. Life is better today. I'm still in diapers, which makes me mad. But now, Nick knows he is being watched.

I learned a lot about Nick this morning. While I was watching TV, he got a phone call. He told his friend about the last few weeks. He lost his job and is in trouble.

His job was to go to grocery stores and set up the rows of snacks—pretzels, chips, and popcorn. He had to make sure the shelves looked good and were full. He took out the bags that were too old and put in the new ones.

Nick lost his job because he was stealing. He took the new snacks off the shelf, not just the old. Then, he sold the snacks to friends. He sold the snacks for less than the store price. When the company found out, he lied. Nick said he was giving the old snacks to the poor. But the company followed him. They saw him selling the snacks.

When Nick's girlfriend found out about it, she left him. He came home and the house was empty. She said if his company didn't tell the police he was stealing, she would. To stop her, he had to pay her money. She owned half their house. He had to buy her half right away. He took money from some bad guys to pay her. The bad guys want their money back...now. That was the phone call he made after the Social Security office. He's in big trouble.

But it's good news for me. Nita won't let me stay with someone who breaks the law.

Chapter 14

Nick has a plan. He always has a plan. It's never a good plan, but he always has one.

Nick calls Bess Wakeling. She is the accountant for my special needs trust. She handles all the money. Nick tells her I'm living with him now. He is going to take care of my money. Bess laughs so hard I hear her across the room.

People with disabilities have things stolen from them a lot. It scared my parents to think it might happen to me. My parents were careful.

To get money from the special needs trust, an accountant says "yes" or "no." If "yes," she will send money to a company. She will not send money to a person. She will not send money to Nick.

My aides have a credit card to buy things for me. Each month, they show the accountant how the money was spent. The accountant will not let them spend too much. My aides are good, though. Nita is a good person. She spends the money to take me to my favorite places, like baseball games.

Nick is walking back and forth. He's holding his head. Bess must have told Nick he can't run the trust. Then his face goes soft.

"Sorry," he tells Bess. "I am Sam's guardian. I thought that means I take care of Sam *and* his money. I want to take Sam on a vacation. We are going to an amusement park. Please send me $20,000 for our trip."

Again, Bess laughs. "Sorry, Nick. It doesn't work that way. That's great that you want to take Sam on vacation. Please write up a plan and send it to me. The plan must show all the costs. If it looks good, I will pay the money to a company. Do you need the name of a good travel agent?"

"But what if I need money on the trip?" Nick says.

"Didn't Sam's home give you his credit card?"

"No, I didn't know there was a credit card." Nick stops walking. I can tell he is happy about the credit card.

"Did they go over the list of Sam's things?"

"No." Nick is walking around again.

"That's very strange, Nick. They must keep a list. I will call them to find out what is going on."

Of course there is a list. If Nick talked with the aides, he would know that. But no, he just took me.

The list is important. One or two times a year, the accountant comes to my home. It's a surprise. She doesn't tell them she's coming. She looks at the list and makes sure my things are still there. People won't steal from me because of the list. I hope the accountant comes to Nick's house. She will know something is wrong.

"Thank you," Nick says. His voice is quiet. He knows his plan won't work.

"I'll call you soon, Nick. Please get me that plan for your vacation. Have a nice day."

Nick throws his phone down. He bends over shaking his head.

This won't be easy for you, brother.

Chapter 15

Nick left the house a few minutes ago. I hear footsteps on the porch. Lanie walks by the window. She knocks and opens the door.

"Hi, Sam. I saw Nick leave. I thought you might be alone. Can I sit with you? Maybe you and I can get to know each other a little better."

She takes the towel off the basket she brought. It's full of cookies with happy faces.

Well, if your cookies taste as good as your banana bread, then please come sit, Lanie!

She sits down next to me and starts talking.

"I woke up today in such a good mood!" She points to a cookie with a smiling face. "So, I made some cookies." She places a cookie on the couch to my left. "Making cookies makes me happy!" She points to the smiling cookie again.

"But my cat kept jumping up on the counter." She turns one of the cookies so the smiling face now looks sad. She points to it and makes a sad face.

"And then my cat—his name is Mr. Whiskers—knocked over the bag of flour." She places the sad cookie to my right and points at it again.

"I love my cat." She points at the happy cookie. "But he is trouble!" She points at the sad cookie.

I see what she is doing. God love this woman.

"Are you happy, Sam?" I move my arm toward the sad cookie.

"Do you like living here?" I try to move my arm closer to the sad cookie.

"Do you want to go back to Michigan?" I move my left arm toward the happy cookie.

I feel like a child, but I'm happy to be able to speak.

"Nick is not always a nice person," Lanie says.

I make a sound and move my hand to the sad cookie.

"His girlfriend told me about him. Nick has been lying to her about a lot of things. She wanted to leave. But this house was hers, too. When he was caught stealing, that was it. She left. I told her you were here. She told me to be careful. She said Nick was up to something."

Hmmm. So, Lanie isn't the nosy neighbor. She is watching out for me.

Just then, the doorbell rings. Lanie gets up to answer it. Well, maybe she is nosy after all.

"Is Sam Jackson here?"

"Yes, come in," Lanie says like it's her house. "This is Sam." She points to me.

"Sam, you are served." Lanie puts her hand over her mouth. The man hands me a thick letter.

"What's this about?" Lanie takes the letter from the man.

"I don't know, lady. I'm just the delivery guy." He turns and leaves. Lanie closes the door.

"Should we open it, Sam?"

I make a sound and touch the happy cookie.

"It's a letter from the court. Someone named Nita Rhodes wants you back in Michigan."

Yes! I knew she would fix this!

"You have to go to court this Friday."

Show me the papers, Lanie! I can read! I want to see what it says for myself.

"This is good news, Sam. Would you like me to be there at court?"

I make a sound. Lanie watches me as I touch the happy cookie.

I don't know what will happen in court. But I need someone on my side. I hope Lanie comes.

Chapter 16

Something is up today. Nick gave me a bath, shaved me, and put me in nice clothes. He even cooked breakfast. Now I am sitting in my wheelchair watching TV. A cooking show is on. It's better than nothing.

Knock. Knock. Knock. Someone is at the door. This house is busy as a bee! Nick opens the door.

"Nick? Tom Cardine." The man shakes Nick's hand. He is tall, like me, and wearing a dark suit.

"Come in." Nick turns and points to me. "This is Sam."

"Hi, Sam. My name is Tom." He puts a card with his name on my tray. "I'm an attorney. The court sent me to help you." Tom speaks loud and slow. Does he think I can't hear? Tom turns to Nick. "Can you give us some time alone? I need to talk to Sam by myself."

"But Sam doesn't talk." I hear Nick's voice crack.

"I know, but I must meet with him on my own."

Move it, brother. I have rights. Get out.

Nick doesn't look well. He walks down the hall. His bedroom door shuts. Tom sits down next to me.

"Sam, a letter was sent to court. The home in Michigan wants you back. They say you didn't want to leave."

I yell and shake my head.

"We go to court tomorrow. I know this is fast. They think you are in danger."

They are right! I yell and hit my tray.

"Don't worry, Sam. We will make sure you stay with Nick."

Wait. What?

"I had a good talk with your brother yesterday. He loves you very much. He is happy you are here with him."

Are you a piano, Tom Cardine? Because you are being played like one.

"Your brother thinks the people at your last home are trying to get your money. I think so too. Living with your brother is what's best. I will say that to the court. It's always better to stay together. That's what families do!"

You fool. Who says it's better? No one who has met my brother thinks so. Not his girlfriend. Not Lanie. Not even my parents.

I can't breathe. My heart beats in my ears. I scream. I hit my tray. I rock my body. My wheelchair hits the table. A glass falls to the floor and breaks.

Nick runs into the room. Attorney Tom just stares with his mouth open.

"Hey, Sam." Nick puts a hand on me. But I won't stop. I won't let this happen to me. I scream. I rock. I hit the tray. Louder. Harder.

Attorney Tom stands up. He's moving to the door.

"It will be OK, Sam. Nick, I'll see you tomorrow."

It will not be OK.

Chapter 17

My brother rolls me into the courtroom. He stops when he sees Lanie. I
wish I could see his face. He doesn't say
"hi," just pushes me to a row of tables.
Attorney Tom walks toward us. He
shakes Nick's hand.

"Nice to see you, Nick. Did you
have any trouble finding the courtroom?"

Hello! Down here! I'm your client!
Attorney Tom hears my sounds and
looks down. I put out my hand to
shake. Attorney Tom pats my shoulder.

"It will be all right, Sam. You'll be
home with your brother soon."

Then he turns and joins a group of
men talking across the room. The men

are wearing the same dark suit as Attorney Tom. The group is smiling, laughing.

So, this is a joke to you. Just another day at work. My rights and my life are in danger.

I make a loud sound. The "suits" look at me. Then they quickly look away. I yell again.

Look at me! I'm the reason we're here today.

The "suits" look uncomfortable and sit down.

A man at the front of the room says, "All rise."

All rise? I'm in a wheelchair. I can't stand up. I can see already that I won't be treated fairly.

The judge walks in wearing a long black robe. She has curly brown hair and is not smiling. She looks like she doesn't want to be here.

"Be seated," says the judge. "We are here this morning to hear the emergency case of Sam P. Jackson, an incapacitated person, case number 160-25."

Incapacitated? That means I can't do anything on my own. I'm not incapacitated. I just need some help doing things.

The judge explains how court will work. Then she calls Nita Rhodes to speak.

Nita! She is speaking through a TV. She tells the judge about my time in the group home. Nita explains that Nick wouldn't listen to my care plan. That he left without the iPad I need to talk.

"Your honor, Sam was doing well here. We are scared for him. We ask the court to let Sam return to his home with us in Michigan."

"Thank you, Ms. Rhodes. Mr. Cardine, you may speak."

Attorney Tom gets up. He tells the judge about my Social Security payments and my special needs trust. He says Nita and the group home are trying to take my money. Attorney Tom points to Nick.

"Nick is a loving brother. He wants to care for Sam. Your honor, I ask that you say "no" to the group home. Sam should live with family. Please keep them together."

What a load of poop. The judge must smell these lies.

"Thank you," the judge starts. "Nick Jackson is Sam's legal guardian, right?" Nick and Tom nod their heads. "Nick has the right to make all decisions for Sam, including where Sam is to live."

"Your honor," Nita speaks up. "For ten years, Nick never came to see his brother. He doesn't call or send presents for his birthday or Christmas."

"Ms. Rhodes, it's not your turn to speak." The judge is mad. "Families should be together."

I can't listen to this trash for another minute. I start to yell and rock my body. Over and over, I hit the tray on my wheelchair. If Nita could see me, she would know I was saying, "No! No! No!" Everyone in the court room is looking at me. But I won't stop. I keep yelling and hitting.

"Your honor, my client is upset. Can we take break?" Attorney Tom says quickly.

"Yes, let's take a twenty-minute break." The judge hits her gavel.

Chapter 18

Bess, the accountant, walks in the courtroom.

"Hi, Sam, it's nice to see you. I'm sorry I didn't get here sooner. My plane was late." She turns to Attorney Tom. "You must be Sam's attorney. We need to talk." She points out the door. This woman is in charge!

When Attorney Tom comes back in, he looks scared. He doesn't talk, just sits down next to me.

"All rise." The judge walks in and tells us to sit.

"Mr. Cardine, is your client feeling better?"

"Yes, your honor," answers Attorney Tom.

Funny, he never asked me how I felt.

"Your honor, the accountant for Sam's special needs trust is here. She would like to say a few words."

Bess tells the judge how my special needs trust works. She says Nita Rhodes and her aides are good people. They follow the rules and do their job well.

"When I make surprise visits," she tells the judge, "Everything is in order. Sam is happy living there."

"Do you believe we are here about money?" asks Attorney Tom.

"I do. But it's not what you've been told." The accountant tells the judge that Nick tried to take over Sam's special needs trust. When he couldn't, he asked for $20,000. "The group home has never asked for money like that."

The judge rests her head in her hand. She looks frustrated.

"This case is about what is best for Sam," says the judge. "The accountant is keeping Sam's money safe. Nick is asking for the chance to care for Sam. He should be given that chance. I believe family should stay together."

Through the TV, Nita yells, "Sam has needs that aren't being met. You aren't letting him talk! He has rights!"

Go, Nita!

The judge's lips are tight. Her eyes are angry.

"Stop, Ms. Rhodes. Nick can learn how to meet Sam's needs. Sam should be with family."

Now I am *really* worried.

Chapter 19

Bess stands up.

"Your honor, Sam uses an iPad to talk. He doesn't have his iPad now. We need to hear from him what he wants."

"Judge, if I may?" Everyone turns to look. Lanie stands and walks toward me.

"Ma'am, sit down," orders the judge.

Out of her purse Lanie pulls her happy face cookies. She places the sad cookie to my right and the happy to the left.

"Sam, which cookie means 'yes?'"

I move my left arm toward the happy cookie. The judge bangs the gavel, but Lanie keeps going.

"Sam, which cookie means 'no?'"
I move my right arm toward the sad cookie.

"Sam, do you want to go back to Michigan?" Lanie asks. I move my left arm toward the happy cookie.

The judge bangs her gavel again.

"Sit down, ma'am. Pointing at cookies is not speech. Sit down. This court is not a game!"

"Sam, do you want to live with Nick?" Lanie asks loudly over the gavel.

I yell as loud as I can. I hit the sad cookie so hard it smashes to pieces.

"Your honor, Sam has told you what he wants," the accountant says as she sits down.

Attorney Tom looks at me. He *really* looks at me. His face is different. Maybe he is thinking about how I yelled when he came to Nick's house.

Then he looks at Nick. Nick is stunned. It's like he has never seen me before. A few seconds go by. Tears come into his eyes.

Quietly, Nick says, "Let him go."

Attorney Tom looks back at me. He stands.

"Your honor, the law says we must do what is best for Sam. Sam doesn't want to live with Nick."

The judge looks really angry now.

"Mr. Cardine, are you saying you are changing your mind?"

"Yes, your honor. Sam's home is in Michigan."

The room is quiet for a long time. The judge has her head in her hands. She sighs and looks up.

"Sam, I'm not going to make you do something you don't want. You can move back to Michigan."

Yes!

"But..."

No, no, no. There is no "but."

"Sam should visit with Nick. Brothers should be together. I hope the group home will work to make that happen."

The judge hits the gavel.

I'm free. I hope.

Chapter 20

I'm home.

Bess and I flew back to Michigan. It was my first time on an airplane. There was a big "Welcome home, Sam!" sign on the door. The hallway was filled with balloons. Nita ran out and gave me a big hug. She spun me around until I almost threw up.

Nita put up some new pictures in my room. They are pictures of the college in town. She knows I'm smart. She always says I should go to college. Maybe I will. Maybe I'll be an attorney someday.

Nick is still my guardian and can make the rules. It isn't fair. But I have a strong circle of support—people who will keep me safe. I also don't think Nick will try something like that again. I saw something different in my brother in that courtroom. Something I did not expect.

After court, he carefully packed my clothes into a bag. Then Nick asked Bess if he could use some of the trust money to come visit me. He said now that my parents are away, maybe we could spend Christmas together. Bess said yes, but only if I want Nick to visit. I am thinking about it.

The funny thing is, Nick has started texting me. And he thought I couldn't communicate! Our texts go like this:

Nick: Hey Sam. How R U?

Me: Well, I'm not in UR ugly brown house, so...GOOD! 😅

Nick: I'm sorry about that, Sam.

Me: Send me some of Lanie's cookies and maybe I'll forgive U.

Nick: I'll see what I can do.

It feels good to be back. I turn on my iPad and listen to The Stones.

Home sweet home.

aide—a person who acts as a helper

accountant—a person who keeps track of money

agent—a person who helps people get things done

attorney—a person who helps people understand the law and goes with them to court

cerebral palsy—a kind of disability that affects how someone moves

gavel—a small hammer made of wood that is used to call for attention

quesadilla—a sandwich made with tortillas and cheese that is cooked

Representative Payee—a person who takes care of the money received

from Social Security for people who
are disabled

to be served—a process used to tell
people they have to go to court

Social Security office—an office of the
US government that gives benefits,
like money, to people who are disabled or retired

Special Needs Trust—an agreement
where one person holds and takes
care of the money for a person who
is disabled

wheelchair—a chair with wheels that
helps people with disabilities move
around

Acknowledgments

This story is a work of fiction, but the goodness of Nita and Lanie were inspired by real people in my life. Their love, care, and support so many years ago have stayed with me.

The YouTube™ influencers Bradley Heaven and Zach Anner helped me learn about life with cerebral palsy. I recommend checking them out on social media.

Thank you, Patrick, Juilene, and Steve for believing this story had legs and helping me develop Sam's creative side.

Many thanks to my early readers for making sure this story made sense and was readable.

To June, who made it possible to have time to write, I thank you.

The cookies in the story are a nod to the PWG. They suffered through my early work and led me to where I am today. "Thank you" is not enough.

And to Isabella, my best beta reader and hero. I love you.